JUNA

Laura Licker

PublishAmerica
Baltimore

ISBN: 978-1-61582-717-6
PUBLISHED BY PUBLISHAMERICA, LLLP
www.publishamerica.com
Baltimore

Printed in the United States of America

JUNA

Laura Licker

⠒

Thank you Sy, for all of the love you have given to me over so many years. Also for teaching me what life is all about. All my love to you forever.

To Sarah, thank you for always being there when I need you. You are a big part of my life and an "adopted" member of my family. I would be lost without you. Tons of love always.

I watch the men all walk by with their hunting dogs. Far below me they are from where I am perched high in the tree. Their voices nothing but murmurs from this distance but their minds are running on overdrive. They all have the same thought. They want nothing but to totally destroy me. My death will not be enough, they want every part of me torn to pieces.

Why do I feel so much hostility and hatred coming from everyone? I pose no threat to anyone. I always keep to myself and never speak a word to anyone I cross paths with. All I ever see is fear in their eyes. I am an outsider, who they do not trust. I am different from all of them and something they will never understand.

I never want to cause pain for anyone or to change their lives in any way. But now, everything is different. I was sent here on a mission for my people. Leela gave me new life, a life worth living.

The homeland was quiet and the Zi'ods were content with how their life was until everything changed. The Zi'ods are peaceful beings that wish to live free as they choose. They do not like conflict or to be told how to live. For many moons the homeland was peaceful. The Zi'ods were happy and fulfilled with life.

They built only what was needed for homes and meeting places. The homeland provided everything they needed. They built things from the trees and plants. The Zi'ods also used water from lakes and grass and dirt from the ground. Their buildings were simple yet effective. They ate from the land. There were plants and animals to sustain them. They wove together items from plants to make their coverings.

The Zi'ods were up and about during the moon. They slept during the sun. Their eyesight is exceptional during the darkness, but they are nearly blind in the light. In the meeting places was where they gathered to socialize with one another. The young and old all liked to play a game called the hunt. This was played quite often.

Their world consisted of limited sound. They do not need to speak, unless they choose to, for they know how to communicate with their thoughts. The sounds you might hear are the animals or the Zi'ods moving about. They do not have sounds from outside sources. The Zi'ods were happy and free. Then one day everything was different.

The Koyds came to the Zi'ods homeland. They wanted nothing but destruction for all Zi'ods. The Koyds saw themselves as superior to all other beings. And therefore, all others must cease to exist.

So the war began. During night and day, there was no rest and no peace for the Zi'ods. The Koyds broke into their homes and dragged the Zi'ods out one by one. The Koyds did not just kill the Zi'ods and be done with it. Instead they found different ways to inflict much pain on the Zi'ods bodies for long periods of time before their deaths would be granted.

Some of the methods of pain would include ripping chunks of hair out, which included skin, from the scalp, by way of the Koyds hands. Another pain method was to cut off the fingers at the first knuckle. Or they would rip off the toe nails. The Koyds also used whips on the Zi'ods until their skin was shredded. They also liked to knock out their teeth. Only after much pain would the Koyds kill the Zi'ods. They did this for one simple reason, because they could. For you see, the Koyds were just purely evil beings.

Any techniques the Zi'ods may have to use for survival are useless against the Koyds. No one could ever hide from them.

The Koyds can pick out any being in any setting. So for the Zi'ods, there was no place to hide. During all of this, the Zi'ods did everything they could to fight the Koyds. They had weapons to beat and to cut the Koyds, but the Zi'ods were out numbered. The Koyds were always stronger too. For the few Koyds that were killed, there was always many more. Still the Zi'ods never gave up hope that one day victory would be theirs.

Day after day, there was war. So much death on both sides, but many more for the Zi'ods. They knew they had to do something before there was no more Zi'ods left alive. Certain members of different families were gathered together in one home. This was the home of the Zi'od leader. The leader said the only way any of the Zi'ods would remain alive is to go to different lands. Everyone readily agreed, seeing no other alternative. No one knew where they would end up. So one by one, they were sent away. When there was one Zi'od left, the leader looked at him. They locked eyes for a few moments. Then the leader took a deep breath and told his son that it was with great sadness that he be sent away. The leader also told him that only if any of the Zi'ods survived, one day the leader would make an appearance when he needed him most. The next thing the young Zi'od knew was he was being whisked away to another place, where he was to live for the rest of his life.

My name is Juna. So many years ago, I was born into darkness, with my father being the Zi'od leader. Our homeland was peaceful and thriving. But that was before everything had changed, before the Koyds came.

For as long as I can remember, there has been war between the Zi'ods and the Koyds. We do all we can for our survival. Day after day, we destroy as many Koyds as possible. Swiftly we put them to death. This killing is something we are strongly against but the choice has been taken from us. With this war, it is kill or be killed. The Koyds want nothing except to be the only beings left alive.

Because of this war, our homeland is almost already destroyed. Our homes have been torn apart. Most buildings have been left as ashes. The Koyds have killed off almost all of our food sources.

Little by little, each day our world is slowly disappearing. Our leader has hopes for the Zi'ods that still remain. We must each be sent to new places in hopes that one day we will be stronger and able to live free once again. This is our only chance to avoid extinction.

It brings me great pain to be sent away. I do not want to leave my homeland. I fear I will never see my father again. I question how will any of us survive in a new place? We do not know what dangers await us. It could be that we are trading one death for another, of our people. My father tells me, this is the only choice we have. He tells me, I have a mission. My mission is to stay alive. Stay alive for all of the Zi'ods that have been taken from us. Being alive will be our victory over the Koyds. So with a very heavy heart, I say goodbye to my father. As our eyes lock on one another, our thoughts let it be known what emotions we feel and what words can not express. And with that, I am taken away to a new land.

I do not know how long I was asleep. I do not know how far I traveled. Our traveling is done in an unconscious state of mind. We are put in a deep sleep, for we are told that if we traveled while fully awake, it would shatter our mind into pieces. We awake with no memory of the travel. And we must be resourceful and make our own way in the new lands that we are put in.

Slowly I awake with excruciating pain in my head. Little by little I flex each muscle to assess if there is any damages. I only detect my head pain, but I know in time it will pass. I feel soft air blowing against my skin and I wonder what I am laying on. It feels thick and soft but with a hardness beneath it. I listen for sounds around me, but all I hear is quietness. Slowly I open my eyes and I am greeted with darkness, much to my relief. I am surrounded by trees and plants. A bed of leaves is what I am laying on. It is good that it is dark, for if it was light, I would be almost blind. Our eyes do not adjust well to light. I see no people around this area, but I am still cautious. Slowly I stand up, still looking around.

I decide to pick a direction and start walking. I know I need a place in which I shall live. So as I am walking, I gather up vines and limbs from trees. With the vines, I can make ropes. With the limbs, I can make walls. As time goes by, I know I have covered much of this wooded area in my gathering and the pain in my head subsides. I know I must find a place to sleep, for I am tired and the sun will be up soon.

I decide to go in a different direction to see what I can find. After walking for a while, I come across a small cabin. It is in the middle of no where it seems. I cautiously move closer to it. I can see it has been abandoned. I inspect the structure of the cabin and it is in sound condition, with the exception of small repairs needed. I walk inside and look around. Some more minor repairs needed, but nothing I can not handle. And with that, I decide this will be my new home. As the sun starts making its presents in the sky, I curl up and go to sleep.

ours later is when I awake. I make sure the tree limbs and vines are all gathered in one area just outside of the cabin. I then wander around to see if any other cabins or such were in this wooded area. As I walk around, I find plenty of food sources, so I know getting enough to eat will not be a problem. It is a long time later when I come to the conclusion that no one else uses any of this area. I then go back to the cabin and start seeing to the repairs that need to be done. Some of the repairs can be made with the vines and limbs I have, but for the rest, I will need other items. So I fix what I can and leave the rest to a later time. This is what I work on for the next few moons.

A few days after that, I am awakened by sounds out in the woods. I immediately go still and listen for a few moments. There are voices I hear and they are getting closer to the cabin. They seem to stop outside for a short time and then move on. After that I hear no one else. I now know there are people in this area and I must venture farther out through the woods to see just how far away they are. So I go back to sleep while I wait for the next moon.

When I wake up, I leave the cabin and find some food to eat. I pick some fruit from the trees. I also pick some berries from the vines. Once my body has some nourishment, I set out through the woods. I walk for quite a while.

I then start to see buildings. There are also plenty of people out and about around this area. This seems to be the main area for public buildings. I walk among all of the people. Most do not seem to take much notice of me other than to have a look of being frightened in their eyes. Some, on the other hand, seem a bit angered by my being here. Most likely due to the fact that I am an outsider to this area.

Some time after I have been in this main area for a while, I start to see that there are less people out. I decide then it is time for me to go back to the cabin. By the time I get there, I am exhausted and I need sleep.

During the next moon, I venture out into the woods with some different items in which to hold water. I then walk to where I remember seeing a stream and fill the containers. I take them back to the cabin and find places to store them. The stream is not far away so I know I have easy access to a water source. After I am finished with that task, I then walk through the woods and into the town. I go inside a few different buildings and look around. One is filled with different things to eat. I look around at a few things out of curiosity and then leave.

Another building has many different items that seem to be for building things. Some of these items I know I could make use of easily. I watch a few people pick out some things and I see that they take them to the person behind a counter. I then see the people make an exchange with the items and something with writing on it.

After watching this for a few times, from different people, I now know that I am missing something to be able to make these exchanges. I am not concerned with this, for I can make everything I need from the woods. Having these items would have just made it easier. I then decide to return to my cabin and start the work I need to do.

For many moons, I work on building things for the cabin. I make a comfortable place to sleep. I also make things I can sit down on. I weave together different things from plants to make many coverings to wear. I also finish the rest of the repairs that needed to be done on the cabin. It feels good to work with my hands and create things. I work from when the moon rises in the sky until it starts to fade away. I sleep in between those times.

When the time came that I woke up with no work to do, I venture out to the stream and decide to spend some time relaxing in it. It is plenty deep enough to sit in comfortably . The water is soothing and feels cool to my warm skin. It is a beautiful night to enjoy.

I have been laying back, soaking in the water when I feel something touch against me. It is my reaction to move quickly away before thinking, since it has startled me. I open my eyes as I sit up and see a young woman sitting there looking at me. Between the two of us, I do not know who seems more surprised by the other. We sit there for a few moments looking at each other without saying a word. Her thoughts seem to be jumbled and not making sense. I can also see sadness in her eyes. I decide to wait and let her speak first.

When she finds her words, she first asks how it could be that she did not see me before she sat down. I simply told her it was one of the things I could do. This seems to puzzle her more. I reply with telling her that I can not be seen if I choose not to be. I know she still does not understand. I decide to change the subject and ask her a question.

I ask her why she has sadness. She immediately wipes her hands across her eyes and says that she must look a mess. I told her no she just looks sad. With that she looks at me and smiles. Her smile reaches her eyes and they are the most beautiful eyes I have ever seen. I know that I will never forget those eyes as long as I live.

She asks me if I come out here often and I tell her I live in the cabin not far from here. She looks at me confused and asks if I mean the old run down hunters cabin. Before I could say anything she said that was the only cabin out here but that it had been abandoned years ago. I simply say that I live there now.

She then asks me if she could visit me there sometime. I told her she could if she wishes to. She smiles and says she would see me again soon but for now it was time for her to go. We both say good night and she leaves. I then walk back to the cabin and decide to sleep.

For the next few moons, I spend time either wandering the woods or enjoying time down by the stream. It keeps me active, with this walking that I do. It also eases my mind by listening to the natural sounds around me. The rest of the time my mind feels distress with worry for my people. I am afraid for all who was left behind. I am also frightened I will never see any of them again. I know to feel this way is useless. It is out of my control. There is nothing I can do to change things. Spending time in the stream is very enjoyable. The water is soothing and relaxes me. My skin is forever warm and the water cools me.

During all of this time, I have no interaction with anyone from the town. No one has been out in these woods. Also I have stayed away from town, for I feel I am not welcomed there, from the looks I have received from the people. I keep to myself for I feel it is important to my survival.

I wonder if I will ever see the young woman again, for I am curious about her. She is the only person I have spoken to. She is different from everyone else, as far as how she reacts to me. I sense no fear or anger from her. I wonder why she is so different.

Many moons later is when I finally see her again. I am in my cabin preparing some food to eat, for I am hungry. I hear movement outside and I go into a defensive mode. The next sound I hear is that of the door slowly opening. I immediately go still. She walks in and quietly closes the door behind her.

She stands there for a few moments waiting for her eyes to adjust. With the moon high in the sky, it is brighter outside than in the cabin. Cautiously the young woman starts to move around. Silently I watch her. It seems as if she belongs here some how. She walks over to a wall and opens the hatch, letting the moonlight inside. She is comfortable in these surroundings. It does not bother me to see her touch my belongings. My eyes never move, but I see everything she does.

She makes her way over to the area of where I am standing. Still I do not move. She walks behind me and then takes a step back. I hear her sharp intake of breath. Her thoughts register panic and uncertainty but her words come out plain and clear when she asks me to show myself. Of course she does not ask me specifically, but she knows someone is there.

I decide then to show myself. This startles her but she tries not to show it. Before she can ask, I tell her I have the ability to blend into any environment I may be in. She replies with saying that she wished she was able to do that. I ask her why and she tells me because with who her family is, she is watched much more than she would like to be. I give her a questioning look and she tells me her parents are the ones who founded this town. So everything she does is reported back to them. I nod my understanding.

I tell her my name is Juna and I ask her for her name. She replies that her name is Leela. I comment that she is familiar with this cabin. She tells me she has been coming here since it has been abandoned. Leela says she is always at peace here. I make the comment that she is happy with the repairs I made. Before she asks, I tell her I can read peoples thoughts. Leela smiles and says she would have to be careful what she thinks around me. I smile in return. We decide to sit down while we visit and we talk for hours.

Leela tells me that everyone in town has been talking about me. She tells me that people do not like me being here. I ask her why, because I know I have done nothing against anyone. She tells me they do not like outsiders because the last time there were any around this town, all they did was vandalize and destroy things. The people here now believe that all outsiders want to do the same.

I ask Leela why she does not fear me as others do. She looks at me for a moment and then replies by saying that there is something calming about me. I tell her that she feels safe being here with me. She slowly nods and says that she does, but she is not sure as to why she feels this way. I look into her eyes and tell her that she knows I pose no threat to her. She replies with agreeing that is true.

Leela is quiet with her thoughts for a moment. During this time I learn that the previous outsiders to this town also caused great pain to some of the people here, besides just doing damage. Leela has lost someone important to her because that person had taken their own life because of what those outsiders had done to them. I tell Leela that I understand what she has lost, for I have lost important members too.

Our eyes lock on each other for a few moments and neither of us says a word. Quietly Leela stands and walks towards me. Then she sits down next to me and softly touches my cheek with her fingers. I close my eyes for a moment and lean more into her fingers as I enjoy the feel of her skin against mine. I then focus on her eyes once again.

Leela asks me about where I come from and I tell her about my homeland. I tell her about my people, the Zi'ods. I also tell her about the war with the Koyds. I tell Leela about my fear of being the only Zi'od left alive. Leela looks at me and softly says that I am not alone anymore, for I have her in my life now. I

LAURA LICKER

watch her eyes as she says this and I know she means what she says.

I then notice the change in the moonlight and walk over to the wall hatch and quietly close it. This put the cabin into darkness. I turn around and look at Leela. She seems a little confused at first but then understanding shows on her face. She looks at me and says there is a problem with me being out in the light and that is why no one has ever seen me in town during the day. I tell her that in the light I am nearly blind. I also tell her that is why I sleep when the sun is up. Leela nods her understanding.

Slowly Leela stands and walks over to me. Her thoughts tell me that she does not want to leave. Leela fiddles with a string from her coverings, as she looks at the floor, and asks me if she can come back again and visit me. I cover her hands with one of mine to calm her and tell her she is welcome to be here anytime she likes. Leela looks at me then and slowly smiles. She tells me then that she will see me soon and she softly kisses my cheek. I say the words, until then my sweet Leela, to her. She smiles and nods in agreement. And with that, she leaves. I then curl up and go to sleep.

During every moon, it has become regular for Leela to be with me. Every time we are together, we become closer to one another. The closer we become, the harder it is when we have to part. Leela tells me the town is angry that we spend time together. The people say I do not belong here and they want me gone. Leela tells me, now that the people know she spends her

30

time with me, that I have corrupted her and because of that, they want my death.

I tell Leela that I want no harm to ever come to her, especially if it is because of me. But I also tell her that I can not walk away from her or let her go. Leela has become extremely important to me. She has attached herself to my heart. I can no longer have a life without Leela.

So as the moons go by and by, Leela and I learn everything about each other. I tell her about the game the Zi'ods like to play called the hunt. I tell Leela that in this game we have to sense where each other is while the one that is hunted uses their defenses. I also remind her that our defenses are the blending in and being still as stone and to be barely breathing. One person is the hunted while the others are the hunters. The one that finds them becomes the next hunted. Leela and I play a version of this game often. Sometimes I surprise her by starting without her but she is getting better and better with sensing where I am.

Leela is always amazed that no matter what the weather is, my skin temperature is always the same, with a warm feel to it. I tell her that we are made to automatically adjust to always be the same temperature. It is so we will be comfortable in any environment. We have many differences but yet in many ways we are the same.

During one of the moons when Leela comes to be with me, she is very upset. Her face is wet with tears. I immediately take her in my arms and ask her what has caused this sadness. She tells me she has had enough of fighting with her parents. I ask her why there is fighting.

She tells me her parents want her to have nothing to do with me. They told her that she is going against the town and the people will not stand for it. They told her that as long as she is with me, then she is in danger. Leela tells me that she could not and will not give me up. We look at each other then and lock eyes. Without either of us saying a word, we both know the depth of the love we feel for one another. We then lean together and experience our first kiss.

Shortly after that, I could see that Leela was tired. I carry her over to the bed and gently lay her down. For a long time, I watch her sleep. I soon fall asleep sometime after I have noticed the moon start to drop from the sky.

For the next few moons, I have no contact with Leela. I do not see her at all. I have no idea as to why this is happening, but I do not like it. It comes to the point where I decide to go into town to see what I can find out. I use my abilities to not be noticed.

While I wander through town, I hear people talking about what they should do about the one out in the woods and I know they mean me. By knowing their thoughts, I know they will not rest until I am destroyed. I finally hear her name and I pay close attention. The people are talking about Leela and they say her parents sent her away to teach her a lesson about not listening to them when they told her to stay away from me. I do not like the sound of this. I also do not like not knowing if Leela is alright.

While I am concentrating on what the people are saying, I slip up in trying to remain unnoticed. Someone walking by bumps into me. They look confused because they can not see me, but they know someone is there. They start talking to the people close to me and everyone starts to panic. During this time, a couple more people bump into me. Some then start to say that the evil from the woods is among them. They start to throw objects in my direction and I am hit by a few. At that time, I flee the area and go back to the cabin.

Once I am safe in the cabin, I notice some sore spots on my body from where things hit me. I decide then that I will never return to town. I also realize that it is only a matter of time before the danger reaches the cabin. As I lay down ready to sleep, I think of Leela. I hope she returns to me soon, for I am lonely without her.

For the next few moons, I keep to myself. I go out into the woods for food when I am hungry. Sometimes I also go for walks in the woods. The rest of the time, I stay in the cabin. I think about Leela most of the time. I miss her as if a part of myself is gone. I have made a few things for the cabin while I wait for her return.

Sometime after that, more often than not, I am brought out of my sleep by hearing people in the woods. I am more than aware that they do not like my being here. Each time I hear them, they are closer to the cabin. When the days come that the people reach the cabin, they also start to do damage to the cabin. Each moon after this happens, I spend my time making repairs. I tell myself I will not leave here. This is now the only home I know.

During one of the repairs, I receive a great surprise. I can hear her thoughts and I know she is close by. My Leela has returned to me. I hastily finish my work and as I turn around, I see her standing there. We lock eyes together and for a few moments nothing is said between us. I then gather her in my arms and I feel whole again. I ask her if everything is alright and Leela tells me it is, now that she is home with me. Leela tells me she has left her parents home and she will not go back. She says no one will keep us apart anymore. I help carry her things inside the cabin. Leela looks around then looks at me and says we belong together. Sometime after that, we both fall asleep. Everything feels right with Leela curled up in my arms.

As time goes by, Leela and I grow closer and closer to each other. Every day our love grows stronger and stronger. It becomes like a routine to make regular repairs to the cabin that the people create. Leela is now like me in the fact that she never leaves the woods anymore. Over time her eyesight has greatly improved in the moonlight. Leela has also grown accustomed to sleeping while the sun is out. We spend much time out in the woods. We like to make up games to amuse ourselves. Leela has a wonderful laugh that makes me smile every time I hear it. We spend a lot of time down by the stream. We are content with our life together here in the woods.

We do not know how long the people from town will continue to cause damage to our cabin. Leela and I fear that one day it will escalate into something more. We do not know when this will happen, but we believe it will be one day soon. We put these thoughts to the back of our minds and continue to enjoy our life. We have a great love between us and that love will see us through anything we must endure.

Neither Leela nor myself likes to be told how to live or what to do. We both like to decide our own minds. The people from town are trying to change that day after day. The damages to the cabin are getting worse. I feel it is only a matter of time before our life is at risk and we become the hunted.

We have been biding our time, out here in these woods. The people from town are getting more and more restless with me still being here. By now everyone knows that I am not from here and I still do not leave. They know I have certain abilities that they do not understand. They know none of it is of a human nature. I am still a great mystery to everyone. A mystery that is not wanted. It is now to the point that it is not my leaving that the town wants. It is my death that the people would prefer.

No one from town comes out to the woods during the moon. Leela and I know it is fear that keeps them from doing so. While the sun is up, it is a different story. More and more times we are awaken by sounds of people out in the woods. Each time we hear them, they are closer and closer to our cabin. It is their fear that keeps them at a slow pace.

When the people are close enough, I can hear their thoughts. They want to cause me great pain. The people remind me of the Koyds, with the fact that they want to tear me apart. The town also has thoughts that I am only the first of my kind of many more to come. They have strange ideas of what they think will happen to them when more of my kind come here. The people think we will infect them with strange things. They think I have already changed Leela into some odd creature.

Now is the time for Leela and I to take some form of action. We are woken up by voices out in the woods. My natural instinct is to stand my ground and defend the life of Leela. She fears for my life more than her own. Leela tells me that she firmly believes she will be fine. She says the people will not harm her since they do not know the secret we keep between us. Her thoughts tell me she is not as sure of that as she tries to sounds. Leela tells me that if we stay in the cabin together, the people will use her as my weakness. She knows that anything they say or do to Leela, I will react to. She tells me that the people will do things like that to corner me and trap me.

In my mind, I know she is right. I tell her I understand what she is saying but how am I to just walk away and leave her? She pleads with me, begs me to please stay alive for her. She tells me this is the only thing she will ever ask of me. I am torn between what I should do. In the end, I know I will do anything she asks me. No matter how much pain it causes me.

I wait until I know there are people close enough to the cabin to be seen. I try to convince myself that if the people see me, they will follow me. And therefore, leave the cabin alone.

My thinking is, with the cabin being left alone, Leela will stay safe. Hopefully she will then have the chance to escape this area. I then say my goodbyes and run out of the cabin. I run all through the woods and make sure the people follow me away from the cabin. I then start to use my abilities and I am not seen as I am able to climb high up into a big tree.

From up in the tree I watch and wait until I can break free and make my escape. I know I have to find Leela. As I think of her, I remember how I felt when we parted. It gave me great pain to leave her behind. She begged me to go and to save myself. I tried to tell her, there was nothing to save without her. Leela told me we would always be together. She said no matter what, she would find me and we would have our life as one. I kissed her deeply with every emotion I had pouring through me. When I pulled back, I gazed into her eyes and placed my hand flat against her belly. I flexed my fingers against her twice as I said I love you both. Then in a flash, I was gone.

Now here I am, high in the tree. I watch in silence. I know the dogs will not pick up my scent, for I have none. No sound will be heard from me, for I am as still and as steady as a solid wall of stone. I can not be seen for as long as I choose not to be. I am like a chameleon in any environment and as I wish. The only drawback to all of this is my mind is split into two places. I know what the men below are thinking. They want to use Leela as a trap to draw me out. I fear for her safety and when they find out the truth, they will want to destroy her too.

My eyes never move, but they see everything. Although some things are shadowed due to the light. Not a single sound do I make. My breathing is so soft and slow it is almost stopped. As time goes by, darkness falls all around me. As this happens, my eyes are now able to adjust and I am able to see better. I tell myself I should leave and hope that Leela's life is spared. But I know I can not do that. She has become my life. I live and breath for Leela and the gift she has given me.

Suddenly I feel a coldness that goes all the way through me. There is a sharp pain in my head and a shrill sound in my ears. I feel myself falling into a bottomless pit. The last thought I remember is of my one love, Leela.

Slowly I awake and open my eyes. I blink but I can not see anything. There is a heaviness covering me. Where I am and what has happened to me, I do not know. I lay perfectly still, for fear of the unknown that surrounds me. Something slowly shifts next to me. I start to see a small patch of light, steadily it grows bigger. Suddenly I am blinded by the light and I squeeze my eyes shut. The next thing I feel is a tiny hand on my cheek. Then there is more movement around me. I feel warm breath close to my ear and words softly whispered to me. There is a familiar voice calling to me. Telling me to come back to them. That they need me and love me. I would know that voice anywhere, for it is forever etched on my heart. She is my one and only Leela. She calls out an order for all the lights to be turned down and it is quickly done so.

Once again I open my eyes and I immediately focus on her. She smiles at me and softly kisses my cheeks. I reach out my hand and touch her belly. She watches the movement of my hand and then covers it with her own. Slowly she looks at me with a bitter sweet smile. She then tells me I missed the birth of our son. At that moment, the tiny hand returns to my cheek. I turn my head to the other side and I reach out for him. She helps me shift him into my arms. She says this is your son, Lajune. He is three weeks old.

Slowly I gaze over every inch of him. I see my son for the first time and I am overjoyed. Suddenly I am puzzled and I have so many questions for Leela. Where do I begin and how do I ask what I need to know? She sees that I am struggling with my thoughts. Slowly she strokes my cheek with the backs of her fingers. She says she will explain everything to me.

Leela tells me that after I departed from her, she started to have great pains in her belly. She was so frightened and she was not sure what to do. She left our home and made her way over to her parent's house. It took her a while to get through the woods and to the other side of town. By the time she got there, she was in so much pain and discomfort, she could no longer stand. She opened the door and collapsed on the floor. Her parents found her laying there and carefully picked her up. They took her into one of the bedrooms and laid her down. She was burning with fever. They removed her shoes and covered her face and neck with cold wet cloths. They also called for a doctor. When the doctor got there, he examined every inch of her. He then diagnosed her with being in labor. Immediately her parents started to panic. The doctor responded with giving them orders of things to do. Some time after that, the baby was born. There were no complications. Leela and the baby were perfectly fine and healthy.

At first Leela's parents do not know how they should react to all of this. There is no doubt as to who the father is. And when the people of town find out there is a baby, they will want Leela dead too. It is not as if they do not like him, they do not even know him. They can not understand why Leela is with an outsider. And what makes things worse is the fact that he is from another world. The town wants death to anyone who does not belong and all who are involved with them. It was from other people in town that her parents found out Leela is with him. They did not approve and they feared for her life. They tried to forbid her from seeing him, to which Leela refused. That was when Leela moved out of her parent's home and vowed never to return unless they changed their ways.

It has been months since the last time they saw Leela. There has been a great emptiness since she left home. Now here she was needing their help, for she had no where else to go. They look at their grandchild and nothing can stop them from falling in love with him. All of their love for Leela also comes back full force. They know they have to get them both far away, out of town. They decide to pack up while Leela and the baby rest.

Some time after that, Leela awakes with a start. She knows she has to find him as fast as she can. Leela knows he is surrounded by danger. Her parents see her moving about the room and make her stop and sit down. Leela then explains to them what needs to be done. Her parents look at each other and they know they would do anything for her. They can not bare the thought of losing Leela ever again. They call to some of their workers. The workers are told by Leela where to find him. Her parents insist that she go with them to their other house, instead of going with the workers. That does not sit well with Leela but in the end she is too weak to argue.

Sometime later, Leela was never sure just how long it actually was, she wakes up in another bed, in another room, in the other house. Her parents walk in, carrying the baby. They sit down on the bed next to Leela and ask her the baby's name. Leela took one look at the baby and said his name is Lajune. She then looks at her parents and asks them where is his father. They hand her the baby and tell her he is in the next room. Leela holds the baby close to her as she stands up and walks out of the room.

For the next three weeks, Leela stays on his bed with him and his baby. Her parents keep a constant watch over all of them, with their workers seeing to their every need. During that time, a stranger shows up at their door. No one knows who this is but Leela takes it upon herself to keep everyone away from him. He never speaks a word. Leela knows, somehow in her heart, that he means them no harm. She stays on the bed while he performs his examinations. He communicates with her mind to let her know his findings.

He mesmerizes her with his eyes and lets her know that everything is alright. What happened to Juna is that he went on total shutdown. It is a defense mechanism for when the mind and heart are at odds with reality. He knew the baby was not due to be born for three more months. And he knew there were no problems with you being pregnant. But knowing the pain you went through and feeling it himself was something he did not understand. Everything he knew was telling him something different. The only reason he could come up with for your pain was because you were being ripped apart by death.

The stranger explains that they only love once in their life and with believing Leela was with in the grip of death, he wanted nothing more but to die with her. So he shut down and waited. Any of the hunters that may have seen him, left him, believing he was dead and it was over and done. The stranger explains to Leela that it would take some time but he would return to her when he could be whole again. He says to keep him surrounded by her love and the love of the baby, for that is what will bring him back. Then in the blink of an eye, the stranger is gone.

Leela also tells me, that since the people were most concerned with dealing with my demise first, that by the time they thought about her, she had delivered the baby. And then her parents had taken them to their other house, which no one in town knows about because it is located in a completely different town. Also no one from town has seen her since she moved out to the cabin, so no one ever knew about her being pregnant. Therefore, they know nothing about the baby.

All the while Leela is explaining all of this to me, I am holding our son and I see every emotion play across Leela's face. My love for her grows deeper with each passing moment. Leela then leans over and kisses me. I hungrily return her kiss. As we slowly break apart, I ask her what the stranger said about Lajune. Leela says he told her he is very pleased with the baby. And the stranger wishes much happiness with many more to come. I smile and tell her the stranger was my father and she smiles back at me. I gaze into Leela's eyes and we tell each other how much we love one another. I know without a doubt, with the appearance of my father, scattered though we may be, the Zi'ods live on and will forever. We both kiss Lajune on his cheeks and that is the exact moment we are taken away to find the rest of the Zi'ods.